*This book is dedicated to my daughter
and to her "Taterbug".*

I live on a farm

and love to be outdoors.

Come take a walk with me.

When I go on walks

I see butterflies,

bees,

I see a baby calf,

a baby donkey,

a baby deer,

I like to play hide and seek.

Can you see me?

Here I am!